MY BODY!
MY RULES!

Conversations about body safety, consent, self-esteem and respectful relationships

written by Jayneen Sanders

illustrated by Asha Das

My Body! My Rules!
Educate2Empower Publishing an imprint of
UpLoad Publishing Pty Ltd
Victoria Australia
www.upload.com.au

First published in 2020
Text copyright © Jayneen Sanders 2023
Illustration copyright © UpLoad Publishing Pty Ltd 2023
Written by Jayneen Sanders
Illustrations by Asha Das
Designed by Ben Galpin

Jayneen Sanders asserts her right to be identified as the author of this work.
Asha Das asserts her right to be identified as the illustrator of this work.

ISBN: 9781761160479

Disclaimer: The information in this book is advice only written by the author
based on her advocacy in this area, and her experience working with children as
a classroom teacher and mother. The information is not meant to be a substitute
for professional advice. If you are concerned about a child's behavior seek
professional help.

Message from Jayneen Sanders

I have written this book with the hope that many young people in India will now have access to knowledge about their body and what 'consent' actually means. Everyone, everywhere has the right to feel safe and be protected from harm. Knowledge is power and I hope the empowering information in this book will provide young people with tools to make safe life-decisions. I am grateful to have the opportunity to write a book that may be life-changing and empowering for many teenagers and emerging adults.

Jayneen Sanders
Author

EDUCATE2 EMPOWER
PUBLISHING

www.e2epublishing.info

Introduction

This book has been written especially for you. It is an important read on the changes to your body as you move from a child to an adult, how to keep your body safe and how to expect respect from others. I want you to feel empowered with this information and I want you to know that you have the right to be protected and to be safe.

Rights and responsibilities go hand in hand. Children and young adults cannot always protect their rights and interests, and therefore, they may need the help and protection from trusted adults (see page 60 and the back cover of this book). Children and young adults have the right to be protected from mental and physical violence, injustice, negligence, abuse, sexual abuse and other threats.

I also wrote this book so you know what a happy, healthy and respectful relationship looks like because that is what you deserve!

Contents

As we grow from children into adults our bodies and our emotions change

All About You

Your body is growing and changing. These changes are normal and natural. As we grow from children into adults our bodies and our emotions change. One day we may feel happy and the next day we may feel sad. At times we may feel anxious or worried, or believe no one likes or cares about us. These changes are all part of a time we call 'puberty'.

What Is Puberty?

Puberty starts somewhere between 8 and 13 years for girls, and between 9 and 15 years for boys. This extended period explains why some young people still look like children and some don't; even if they are of similar ages. When puberty starts, a special part of the brain releases chemicals called hormones. These hormones spread throughout the body and will cause lots of changes both emotionally and physically.

Boys

For boys, a hormone called testosterone will cause the growth of hair on their body, particularly their face, underarms and around their penis and testicles. Their testicles will drop lower in their body and become bigger, and their voice will start to change from a high tone to a deeper tone. Their penis will also get bigger and wider, and many boys tend to develop wider shoulders. Testosterone is also the chemical needed for men to produce *semen so they can reproduce (be a father to a baby). At this stage, teenagers are inquisitive and may be even infatuated with the opposite sex or someone they know. This is normal and natural but it **does not** mean they need to act upon these urges.

*semen: a white, cloudy liquid coming from the penis which if injected into a female's vagina can fertilise a female's egg to produce a baby. Note: it is normal for boys to have 'wet dreams'. This is where they may get an erection (the penis enlarges) in their sleep, resulting in an orgasm — an experience where semen is ejected.

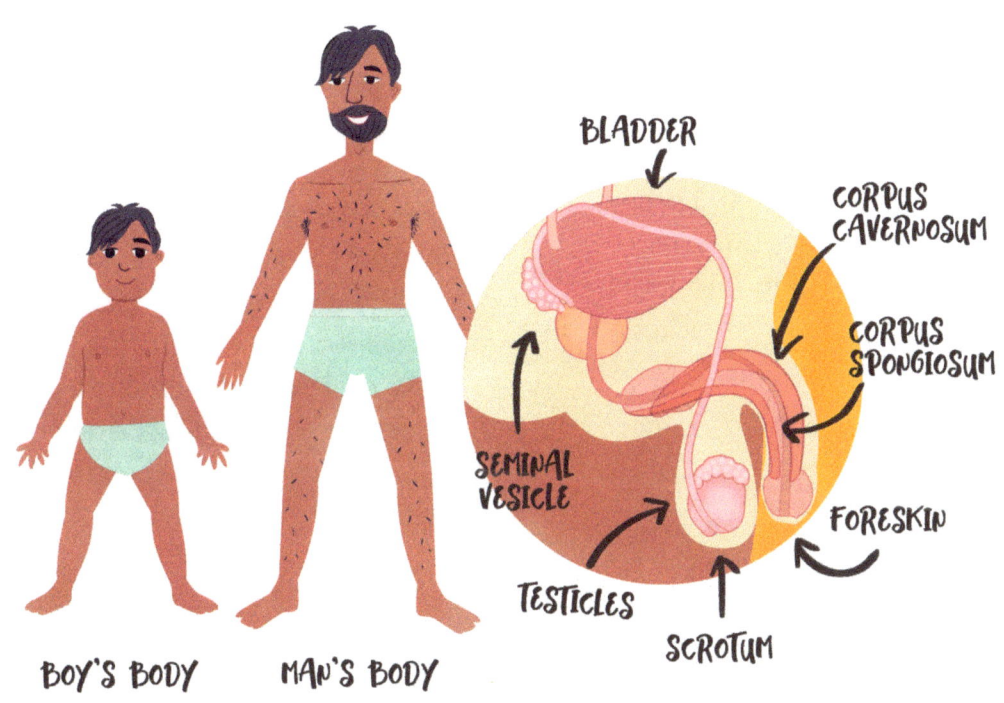

BLADDER

CORPUS CAVERNOSUM

CORPUS SPONGIOSUM

SEMINAL VESICLE

FORESKIN

TESTICLES

SCROTUM

BOY'S BODY

MAN'S BODY

When puberty starts, a special part of the brain releases chemicals called hormones

Girls

During puberty, a girl will grow hair under her arms and around her vulva, and her breasts will start to enlarge. She may also at this time become more interested in the opposite sex and sexual relationships. She may also worry more and more about her appearance and what others think of her.

Hormones will also target a girl's ovaries (which she has had since birth and which contain thousands of unfertilized eggs). Hormones from the brain and the pituitary gland cause the ovaries to start making other hormones called estrogen and progesterone. Together these hormones prepare a girl's body to start her 'period' or 'menstrual cycle'. Having a menstrual cycle will enable a girl to become pregnant if she decides, in the future, to have a baby with her partner.

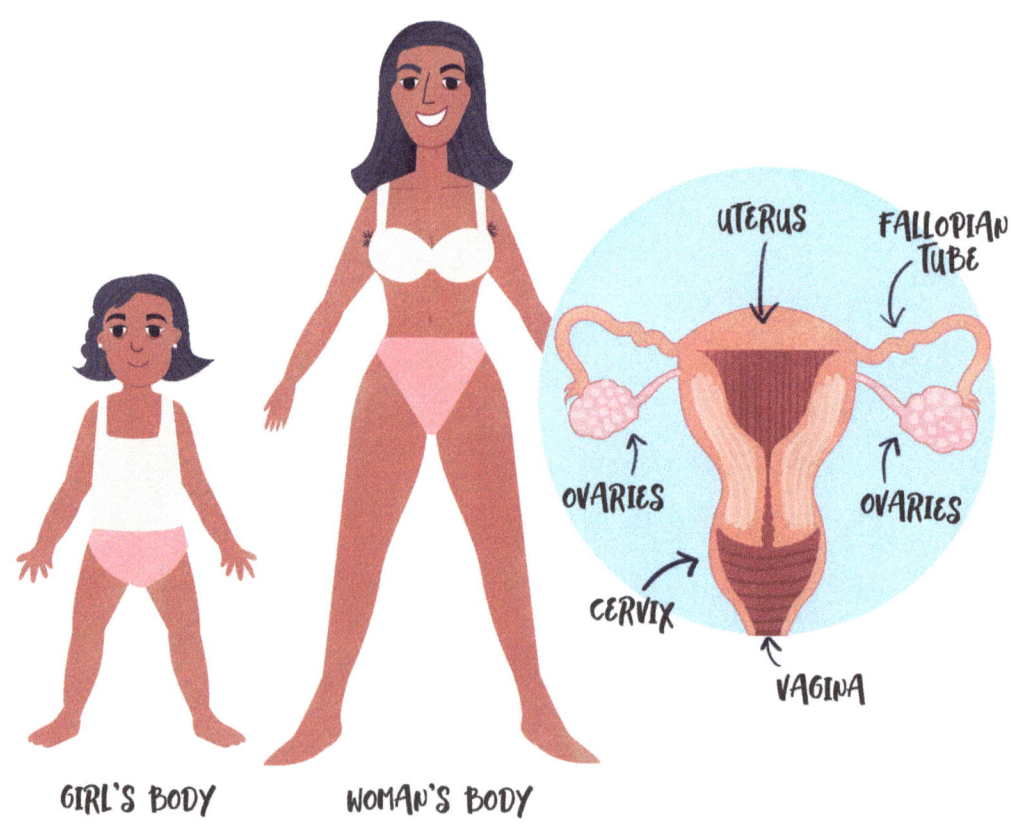

GIRL'S BODY   WOMAN'S BODY

UTERUS   FALLOPIAN TUBE   OVARIES   OVARIES   CERVIX   VAGINA

Girls start menstruating anywhere between 8 and 18 years old. The average age is around 12 years. During menstruation the lining in the wall of a girl's uterus (womb) thickens and then sheds every 28 to 30 days. Girls and women will bleed on average from 3 to 5 days. It's important to note that nothing is wrong with your menstrual cycle if it is a couple of days longer or shorter than this. The heaviness of the bleeding will depend on your body. Some girls and women have a heavy flow and some get a lighter flow. Menstruation is nothing to feel shame or guilt about. It is normal and it is natural for all girls and women between the ages of approximately 8 and 50 years.

DID YOU KNOW?

At the time of puberty, both boys and girls will have a growth spurt and become taller and may even put on weight. Their hair and skin may become oiler and their skin may also break out in pimples. It is normal for both girls and boys to worry about their appearance, but try not to let this worry and overwhelm you. Remember, puberty is a time of change but it is also a normal and natural process.

Private and Public

Private means just for you. A private space may be the bathroom, toilet or your bedroom. Public spaces are shared by many people such as a kitchen or classroom. As you grow older, it is normal to want to explore your own body especially your private parts, but this should only happen in a private space. This kind of exploration is a normal part of growing up and you should never feel ashamed.

DID YOU KNOW?

Your private parts are the parts of your body covered by your underwear. Girls have a vulva on the outside and a vagina on the inside. They have breasts, nipples and a bottom. Boys have a penis, testicles and a bottom. These are your private parts and they belong just to you. No one can touch or look at your private parts without your consent (see page 29 for more information on consent).
Note: your mouth is a private part too!

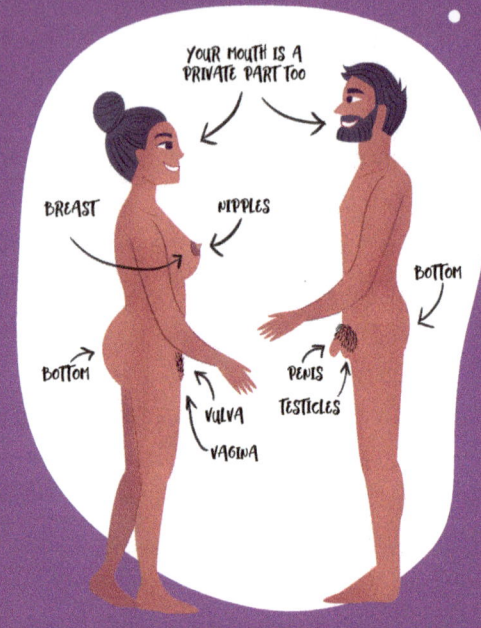

As they grow into adulthood, girls and boys will become more interested in sex and sexual activities with a person they find attractive. Sex is where two people over the age of 18 years enjoy each other's bodies for pleasure, and in time, when they are mature enough, they may engage in sex to produce a baby. Sex is not bad. It is a natural and pleasurable part of life. When two people are in a long-term relationship it is something to enjoy and share together.

Sex is a very serious commitment and one that should not begin before 18. This is because a person before this age is not mature enough to understand the commitment, and their mind and body are not ready for a sexual relationship. Therefore, it is best to find many other great things to do as a teenager such as lots of sport activities, study, and just spending fun time with your friends to burn up your extra energy.

It is very important to note, that in India, it is illegal to have sex with a child under the age of 18 years. This is the law in India, as children under 18 years CANNOT give their consent and are not mature enough to engage in sexual activities.

HAVING SEX BEFORE 18 IS ILLEGAL IN INDIA

Beware of People Trying to Trick You!

People who may be older than you or people who have more power than you (particularly men) or even people who you might trust in normal circumstances, might try to trick you into sex or marriage before you are 18 years old. Your mind and your body are **not** ready for sex and pregnancy before you are 18. As best as you are able, stand up for yourself and say 'No' firmly if you are asked to engage in, or forced into sexual activities. If you can't say 'No' you **must not** feel shame or guilt; just leave quickly and go to a trusted adult for help, or reach out to Childline 1098 or SJPU/Police 100 or DCPU/CWC — they will help you. It is their job to protect children in these types of unsafe situations. So **never** hesitate to get help if you feel concerned or unsure.

Here is another very important point to **always** remember — it is better to wait in your own interests until you are legally and biologically ready to get married or have sex; wait until you have found someone you really trust and love — **this is your right**. It is important to know that it is **illegal** in India to be married before you are 18 years old for girls, and 21 years old for boys.

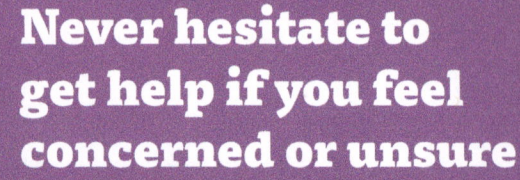

Never hesitate to get help if you feel concerned or unsure

Our feelings are
always changing
and we don't
always know why

Changing Feelings

During your teenage years, you will have many different feelings and emotions. One day you may feel happy, but the next day you may feel anxious or sad. Our feelings are always changing and we don't always know why. You may also feel like people are telling you what to do, and you may feel angry and sad all at the same time! This is all normal and it is natural.

As we learnt on pags 2–5, hormones will be released in your body during puberty. Hormones are not only responsible for changes in your body but they are also responsible for your changing, and often challenging, emotions and mood swings. You might get easily embarrassed and feel like everyone is watching you. You might be ashamed of your body and its changes. You may feel anxious about becoming an adult or you may feel depressed for no reason at all. Growing into a teenager can be a difficult time for all. You can grow up more confidently by sharing your problems with a trusted adult. Never hide your doubts and feelings of confusion, and never try to solve your problems by yourself. Feel confident to always speak up to a trusted adult. It is also important to share your feelings and emotions with your friends, parents and teachers. Keeping a network of trusted and supportive people, such as your mother, father, brother, sister and friends is important. These are the people with whom you can share your feelings and they will offer you supportive advice. If you feel like you can't talk to anyone, there are other organisations you can contact such as Childline 1098. They are there to help you through this challenging time.

Idea!

Why don't you keep a diary and write down how you are feeling every day. Writing things down is a great way to help you understand the thoughts and emotions inside you. Remember if you are feeling sad or anxious, it is also very important you talk to a trusted adult (or a close friend) about these feelings. You should never feel ashamed or guilty about how you are feeling. Everyone, everywhere feels like you at times. It is normal and it is natural.

Even though you are changing from a child into an adult, it is important to keep loving yourself and remain confident

The Importance of Self-esteem

It is important during your teenage years to feel good about yourself. Even though you are changing from a child into an adult, it is important to keep loving yourself and remain confident. This is not always an easy thing to do. Tell yourself every day that you are going to be okay, that you are amazing and unique in your own way, and that you are going to lead a fulfilling life — which is such a blessing! Keep yourself active and engaged in life. Develop a beautiful and meaningful dream and pursue it with all your heart.

However, if you do feel like you are loosing self-confidence, don't be too harsh on yourself. Just as you are kind to others, be kind to yourself. Do not compare yourself with others, you are unique; there are no two similar people in the world. And that's amazing! Girls need to be particularly kind to themselves and to one another. Know that your body is amazing and it is strong, and you are beautiful just the way you are!

So Important

It is **so important** to feel good about yourself. Don't rely on other people admiring you to feel beautiful. Such people may be trying to manipulate you into doing something you shouldn't. For example, a person might tell you that your hair and skin are stunning, just so they can entice you and try to spend more time with you, or get you to do something they want. Be wary of people who are always trying to charm you with compliments. The best person to listen to is yourself! If you feel beautiful and amazing that is all that counts!

Self-esteem Tips

* Stand in front of a mirror and say, 'I am strong, I am smart and I am perfect just the way I am!'

* Follow a passion; it might be drawing, drama or a sport you love.

* If you are having a bad day, speak to a good friend about your worries or simply tell yourself, 'All things pass. Tomorrow will be a better day.'

* Keep a diary of how you are feeling each day. Even if you are having a bad day, try to write down one thing you are grateful for each day.

* List all the great things your body can do; it might be as simple as, 'My arms are perfect for hugging my little sister. I love that my eyes can read and see the beautiful sunset.'

* Tell yourself everyday that you are doing the best you can and that is okay!

Write all the things you like about yourself
in the love heart below.

I have a body boundary. This is the personal space around my body. No one can come inside my body boundary without my permission (consent).

Body Safety

When you were younger you may have learnt these **very** important Body Safety Rules:

1. My body is my body and it belongs to me. I can say 'No!' if I feel unsafe or if don't want to kiss or hug someone. I can give them a high five or shake their hand instead.

2. I have a body boundary. This is the personal space around my body. No one can come inside my body boundary without my permission (consent). If they do, I have the right to say 'No'. If it is difficult for me to say 'No' to this person, I must get away as quickly (GO) as I can and TELL a trusted adult on my Safety Network.

3. I have a Safety Network. These are 3 to 5 adults that I trust. I can tell these people anything and they will support and believe me and help me. If I feel worried, scared or uncomfortable, I can tell someone on my Safety Network how I am feeling and why I feel this way. One person on my Safety Network should not be a family member.

4. If I feel frightened or unsafe I might feel sick in my stomach, get sweaty palms and my heart might beat really fast. These feelings are called my Early Warning Signs. If I feel this way about anything, I need to tell an adult on my Safety Network straightaway.

5. I always call my private parts by their correct names. No one can touch my private parts or ask to see or photograph my private parts. No one can show me their private parts or ask me to touch their private parts. And no one should show me pictures of private parts. If any of these things happen, I need to tell a trusted adult on my Safety Network straightaway.

6. I don't keep secrets only happy surprises that will be told. If some one asks me to keep a secret, I tell them I don't keep secrets. If someone asks me to keep a secret that makes me feel unsafe or uncomfortable I need to tell adult on my Safety Network straightaway! Secrets like those must be told!

7. Always keep a family member or a someone in your Safety Network informed of your whereabouts. Give them an alternative phone number (your friend's number) for them to reach you if you do not come back on time. You could also have a family 'safety' word. If you phone and you say this word, for example, 'coconut' your family will know you need their help straightaway.

And remember! It is **never** too late to tell a trusted adult what has happened to you.

I have a Safety Network.
These are 3 to 5 adults
that I trust.

Write labels and draw the Early Warning Signs
you may get when you feel unsafe.

ACTIVITY PAGE

Write down the names and phone numbers
of the people on your safety network.

Name:
_____

Phone:
_____

Name:
_____

Phone:
_____

Name:
_____

Phone:
_____

Name:
_____

Phone:
_____

Name:
_____

Phone:
_____

Write down the things that may make you
experience your Early Warning Signs.

_____

_____

_____

_____

_____

_____

_____

_____

Now you are older these Body Safety rules **still** apply. One of the most important rules for you to remember is this:

- If you feel unsafe in anyway and your Early Warning Signs begin, **do not** ignore them. Get away from that person or the situation straightaway. Some people may pretend they want to be your friend, but if they come inside your body boundary or touch your private parts without your permission (consent) you have the right to say 'Stop' or 'No' and get away as quickly as possible.

You might find it difficult to say 'No', especially in the following two situations.

1. Maybe the person who is making you feel unsafe is someone in authority; someone who is more powerful than you. This person may threaten or blackmail you, they may deceive or manipulate you or they may just use their powerful position to make you feel unsafe to speak up.

2. The second situation may be a person who you have trusted all along; you may value their relationship and don't want to sever it by saying 'No' — even though you feel unsafe.

STOP

CHILDLINE
1098

This is understandable, but in both situations you will need to be brave. You will need to remember this: **your body is your body, and no one has the right to touch you or make you feel uncomfortable**. So even if you can't say 'Stop' or 'No', don't feel any shame or guilt, just get away as quickly as possible and tell a trusted adult straightaway. A trusted adult is someone who **will** believe you and help you. If you don't have anyone to tell, call Childline 1098. Don't hesitate; it is their job to help you. And remember, that if someone genuinely loves you or cares for you, they will not do anything harmful to you or force you to do something you don't want to do.

Sometimes a person might come inside your body boundary. They might stroke your hair or rub your arm or want to hold your hand. They might think this is okay, but if you don't like it, you have the right to say 'No' or 'Stop'. The person might say they meant no harm, but remember, your body, your rules! So even if a person touches you in a non-sexual way, you **still** have the right to tell them to stop. It is often hard to stand up against some people but you have the right to do so. **Please always remember this.**

Practise standing in a superhero pose. Now draw yourself in the same pose saying 'Stop' or 'No' to another person. You can place your hand out infront of you as the girl does on page 24.

ACTIVITY PAGE

Write down all the things you have learnt
about Body Safety.

You always need to ask for a person's full and clear consent before engaging in any physical contact and a relationship

What Is Consent?

Consent is a very important word. We shall look at this word in two ways.

1. There is 'consent' as in saying 'Yes' if someone asked you if they could borrow your pen or give you a hug to say 'Hello'.

2. Then there is 'sexual consent'. This is saying 'Yes' to sexual activities. *Please note: under Indian law, children under the age of 18 years are NOT LEGALLY competent or able to give consent to sexual activity.*

    Sex with a child before 18 years is a cognizable (or punishable) offense in India.

Consent as in point 1, means you have happily said 'Yes' to something, for example, you have may have said 'Yes' to a hug from your cousin or you may have said 'Yes' to holding a friend's hand when they asked you to. In regards to your body, consent means you are taking a well-informed voluntary choice to say 'Yes' and you have given another person permission to come inside your body boundary.

Now you are growing older, you may be more interested in exploring a physical relationship with another boy or girl. You may feel you'd like to hold their hand, kiss or hug them. However, you can do none of these things if they do not give their consent. You always need to ask for a person's **full and clear consent** before engaging in any physical contact and a relationship.

Note: doctors, nurses, dentists and any healthcare professionals need to ask for your consent before they touch any part of your body. If you are under 18, a trusted adult should be in the room with you if a healthcare professional is examining your private parts for health-related reasons.

This poster shows you the different ways consent **can be given** and the ways it is **not given**.

CONSENT – words and how you say them matter!

NO CONSENT

No!
I don't want to!
Absolutely not!
No way!
Nup!
mmmm...
I don't like that!
I'm not sure
Maybe...
Let me think about it...
You cannot.
Not really.
I don't think so.
Maybe later...
(*Silence*)

CONSENT

Yes!
Absolutely!
I want to do this!
For Sure!
I will allow you to...
It's okay (but in strong voice)
I'm sure!

How you can ask for CONSENT

Can I please...?
May I please...?
Will you let me...?
Would you like to...?
Do you want to...?

Sex with a child before 18 years is a cognizable (or punishable) offense in India

Here are some other ways a person can say 'No'. When they say these things they are **NOT** giving their consent.

ACTIVITY PAGE

Write all the ways you can say 'No' that show you have
NOT given your consent.

ACTIVITY PAGE

Write all the ways you can say 'Yes' that show you
HAVE given your consent.

Here Are the Rules of Sexual Consent After the Age of 18 Years

It is customary in India to restrict sexual intimacy to married relationships, even though legally young people over 18 may make their own choices. Some do choose to have non-married sexual relationships. Because of social disapproval and stigma, they may not find people with whom they can discuss problems in their relationships. One of the problems is that often one partner has forced the other to go further then they want in the area of physical intimacy. This is not good. Even if you have got into a sexual relationship before marriage, it is important to understand these things about consent:

1. Both people are willing and happy about engaging in intimacy or closeness. Each person can check in and say, 'Can I ...?' But no one should be made to feel guilty or pressurized to accept or do things they feel uncomfortable about.

2. You have every right to say 'No' in all circumstances. The other person should never make you feel shameful, guilty or fearful about saying 'No' or 'Stop'.

3. If a person is drunk, has taken drugs, is passed out or is asleep, is under 18 years, and/or has been forced into giving consent, then they **cannot** and **have not** given their consent. If a person does do sexual things when a person is drunk, has taken drugs, passed out or is asleep this is rape.

4. Saying 'Yes' once doesn't mean a person can touch you every time. **You can withdraw consent at anytime**.

5. Silence does not mean 'Yes'.

Consent matters because
it shows you care about
the other person and you
respect them

Why Does Consent Matter?

Note: any sexual relationship, whether there is consent or not, is illegal in India below the age of 18 years. It is a punishable by law.

Consent matters because it shows you care about the other person and you respect them, and you don't want to take advantage of their weakness or trust in you. Without consent, you are asking a person to do something they do not want to do or are unsure about. No one should be forced, deceived or pressurized to do something against their will and be forced into something they feel unsure or uncomfortable about.

Please remember!

If anyone touches you (any physical contact) with sexual intent, it is a punishable offense under Indian law.

For example:

You may say to someone, 'I want to kiss you. Do you want me to kiss you?'

Firstly you have done the right thing and asked for the person's consent. You have shown respect (see more information on respect on page 45). This is the right thing to do.

* If they say 'Yes' enthusiastically and they are very happy about it, then you can kiss them.

* If they say 'Yes' in a timid voice and seem unsure or worried, this is not consent. You could say, 'Are you sure? We don't have to.'

* If they say, 'No', 'I'm not sure', 'I don't know' or there is silence then this is **not** consent and you must stop immediately.

* If they say 'Yes' and you start, and then they pull back and seem worried, then you must stop. They have withdrawn their consent. Check in again to see if everything is okay. Ask, 'Are you okay?' **Do not** put any pressure on the person to agree to do things which they are uncomfortable about or which makes them feel unsafe.

And remember just because a person consented this one time, they may not consent the next time. It is not appropriate for a person to say, 'You did it once, why are you not agreeing now?' Just because you consented once, does not mean you will consent again. Consent is ongoing and should be asked for each time.

If you are the person who is asking someone to kiss you and they aren't consenting, then it is **your** responsibility to stop. Consent does matter! Consent is all about respecting the other person's choice.

Two More Important Points

It does not matter what a person is wearing or what colour they are wearing or what jewellery they have on, or even if they did not disapprove of inviting text messages you sent — if they do not give their consent then you cannot come inside their body boundary. Wearing whatever clothes a person wants is their right. And you have no right to pass judgement on that person. Just because, for example, a girl is dressed in a short skirt and/or they are willing to be out alone and/or travel with boys, does not mean they want any sexual contact. It also means you cannot yell nasty things at them or stare or talk about them in a harmful and disrespectful way.

If you see another person being pushed into something they do not want to do; or someone is touching them and it's obvious they did not give their consent; or they are under 18 years old, do not look away or walk away. Say something if it is safe to do so. You could say, 'Stop. This girl/boy has not given their consent.' If it is not safe to do so, or you feel unsafe also, call the police (Police: 100).

39

Please Remember!

If anyone ever comes inside your body boundary **without** your consent, please remember it is never ever your fault! Even if they falsely say you encouraged them or say other things, you must feel **no** shame or guilt. That is what they want you to feel, but they are actually at fault, and they are responsible for their own actions. Please remember, it is **not** your fault if another person comes inside your body boundary without your consent.

If anyone ever comes inside your body boundary without your consent, please remember it is NEVER ever your fault!

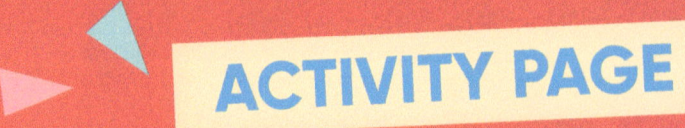

ACTIVITY PAGE

Has CONSENT been given?
Place a tick for 'yes' and an x for 'no' beside each picture.

A

B

C

D

ACTIVITY PAGE

Write why you think the person did or
did not give their consent.

A _____

_____

B _____

_____

C _____

_____

D _____

_____

If you have any questions about consent, write them below.

_____

_____

_____

_____

_____

_____

_____

A respectful relationship does not take advantage of another's vulnerability or loneliness or the need for friendship

What Is a Caring and Respectful Relationship?

Respectful relationships are about valuing people, including those who may look or act differently to you. Respect is about admiring a person and appreciating both their behaviour and actions, and liking them for who they are.

Being in a caring and respectful relationship with another person should be positive for both people, and both people feel valued by the other. A respectful relationship does not take advantage of another's vulnerability or loneliness or the need for friendship. As you grow older, no doubt you will develop a more intimate relationship with a person you care about. This means you will care about the other person's needs rather than trying to get them to fulfil your own needs.

Here are the characteristics of a caring and respectful relationship. Remember, it is your right to have a caring and respectful relationship with a partner.

1. Each person is equal in the relationship. Each gender is equal. No one is more powerful than the other.

2. Both people feel safe and secure with each other. They trust the other person. They feel they have a voice and can speak up if they need to and still remain safe. They can be themselves without fear of rejection. They can communicate about anything.

3. A caring, respectful relationship is also a healthy relationship. Both people want the best for the other and they always encourage them to grow as a person and to follow their goals. They would never hold the other person back from following their dreams.

4. In a caring and respectful relationship each person shows compassion and empathy towards the other. They never judge or correct. They listen and help if they can.

5. Each person in a caring and respectful relationship honours the other person's choices. They do not judge them for their choices. Even if they don't agree, they will not try to change the other person's mind. They do not guilt or shame the other person. There is space in this relationship to respectfully agree or disagree.

6. When engaging in intimate activities such as kissing, hugging and holding hands, one person needs to ask for the other's consent. If it is not given, then nothing can happen. In a caring and respectful relationship each person always asks for the other's consent especially around body boundaries.

7. No one should show any sort of violence to the other. This includes verbal, physical and sexual abuse, as well as threats of violence to another person or family members. They should also **never** stalk or harass. If this happens get away as soon as possible and tell a trusted adult and/or the police.

An unsafe and exploitative relationship can be very dangerous for you

How Do You Know If You Are in an Unsafe Relationship?

An unsafe and exploitative relationship can be very dangerous for you. Here is a checklist of **warning signs** that may help you identify if you are in an unsafe relationship. If you are experiencing some of these warning signs, seek help from the organisations listed on page 60 or the back cover immediately.

Control

- [ ] The person may try to control everything you do. At first they may seem charming and say all the right things, but as time goes on, they try to control your life; they want to know what you are doing and/or who you are with at anytime of the day.

- [ ] They may control yours or the household money.

- [ ] They may stalk (follow) you physically and/or by phone and/or on social media.

- [ ] They gradually start deciding who you should mix with, where you should go, who you should speak to, what you should wear, etc.

- [ ] They may be jealous of your relationship with family and friends, and try to turn you away from them.

- [ ] They may refuse to talk to you about your relationship or important issues, for example, family.

- [ ] They do not trust you and you do not trust them.

- [ ] They may also threaten to harm themselves if you do not do what they ask. They may refuse to eat, cut or injure themselves, write a letter in blood or say they will commit suicide to manipulate you.

- [ ] They may promise you fancy gifts, expensive trips or take you to beautiful restaurants in exchange for a relationship or taking care of them or simply to make you feel obliged to them.

- [ ] They might ask you to go to secluded places without getting the consent of your parents or legal guardian. They may ask you to keep it as a secret and tell no one.

- [ ] They may decide where you are to work or study.

- [ ] They may try to hinder your progress in school, college or work and eventually make you drop out.

- [ ] They may ask you or force you to take and share revealing photos or videos and then they may use these to blackmail you in some way.

- [ ] They may touch you inappropriately and/or threaten you.

Abuse

- [ ] The person may physically hit or kick you.

- [ ] They may shout, scream and/or say verbally abusive things to you.

- [ ] They may sexually assault you. They may force you to do sexual acts when you do not want to.

- [ ] They may force you to watch pornography.

- [ ] They may say things to you to make you feel awful and damage your self-esteem.

- [ ] They may be cruel and unkind to you in secretive ways that others can't see.

- [ ] They may be abusive to you in front of others and make fun of you.

- [ ] They may make fun of and/or are critical of your body, how you look and/or how you dress.

- [ ] They may share details of your personal relationship with friends in a harmful manner and character shame you.

Manipulation

- [ ] The person may try to turn other people against you and tell lies about you.

- [ ] They may manipulate you so you think everything is your fault.

- [ ] They may make you feel like everything you do is not good enough.

- [ ] They may say that they are much more powerful and stronger than you, and that you are a weak and useless person.

- [ ] They may also trick you and say that you are lucky to be with them because no one else would want to be with you (of course this is false).

- They may bully you into doing things that are illegal or against your beliefs.

- They do not tell you where they have been but expect you to always tell them where you have been or where you are going.

- They may compare you to other people to make you feel a lesser person.

- They may insist that you are mad or crazy if you argue back or accuse them of any form of manipulation or abuse. They may say you are imagining it and may threaten to harm themselves if you don't do what they tell you to.

- They may blackmail you by saying that they will disclose your secrets and/or share images of intimate conversations or situations.

- They may encourage you to run away from home with a promise of a good job or marriage.

Inequality

- The person may expect you to do all the work and they do very little.

- They may say that women are not equal to men and that you are a lesser person.

- They may treat you as a lesser person and unequal to them in status in the community and/or family.

- They may treat you as stupid and that you are incapable of trying anything new.

- They may not respect your 'No' and do not ask your consent for anything.

- They may threaten that they are going to leave you, and you will have nothing and be nothing.

Value

- The person may say they only value you for one thing; that might be your looks or ability to make money.

- They don't value your emotions or feelings. They only abuse you and/or make fun of you if you are anxious, scared and/or sad.

- The person does not make you feel good about yourself, and you do not value yourself ever since you have been in the relationship.

- They are often not interested in your work or projects.

- They are often not interested in meeting your friends and family.

- They may make you feel lonely and isolated.

ACTIVITY PAGE

Write a summary of all you have learnt about a
caring and respectful relationship.

ACTIVITY PAGE

Write some of the warning signs of
an unsafe relationship.

Write a summary of what you can do to protect yourself
from an unsafe relationship.

The Internet can be a fun place to be social with your friends, but it can also be a dangerous place

The Internet and Mobile Phones

The Internet can be a fun place to be social with your friends, but it can also be a dangerous place. There can be people on the Internet who are not who they say they are. There can also be images on the Internet of private parts and people performing sexual acts (pornography) with no consent. These images are not suitable for teenagers and in fact, they can be very frightening and portray a false reality. They show relationships that are not respectful, especially to women, and where consent is **not** given. A respectful relationship (see page 45 for more information on respectful relationships) is very different to pornography on the Internet. Therefore it is important you stick to the following rules to help keep you safe from the dangers of the Internet.

DID YOU KNOW?

Watching pornography can be very addictive and can greatly affect your mental health. Research is now telling us that such an addiction can ruin marriages, lead to sexual addiction and/or unhealthy behaviours and encourage sexual aggression. It is best to find other healthier ways to spend your time. This addiction can cause mental harm and affect your future.

Staying Safe on the Internet

Dos

✓ Check with your parents/family before posting personal pictures online on before sending them via a phone or email.

✓ Check and use 'Privacy Settings' on social media sites to protect your privacy.

✓ Tell a trusted adult if someone makes you uncomfortable, scared or confused online.

✓ Meeting someone you know only online can be dangerous. Make sure you inform your parents/family about any such plans/request.

✓ Use strong passwords having alphabets, numbers and special characters so that others can't guess and use your password.

✓ Limit your online friends to people you actually know in real life. Don't accept friend requests from people you don't know.

✓ Play only games that are available on the official app stores or libraries. Also always download apps from the official app stores.

✓ If you see any images of violence, nudity, pornography or content that are not right for your age, close the window immediately. Tell a trusted adult about this immediately.

Don'ts

✖ Do not disclose your personal information like your address, school name, phone number, or current location to people you don't know. This information should never be shared online. Even if your Privacy Settings are High.

✖ Never send pictures or videos online to strangers.

✖ Never open files, games, music or videos sent to you by an unknown person online. It may be a virus or malware.

✖ Do not reply to text, email or pop up messages that ask for personal details.

✖ Do not share your location with strangers.

✖ Do not share your password with anyone, even your friends.

✖ Do not fill out any survey, membership or application form asking for your personal information or request to participate in programmes, games shows, etc.

Adapted from an advertisement by NCPCR, Govt of India.
More details at http://ncpcr.gov.in

Another Important Point

If someone sends unwanted and/or unsafe messages and/or images of their private parts and/or pornography to your mobile phone, block the caller straightaway. This is **not** okay. If someone asks you to send photos of yourself, with or without clothes, or asks you to engage in a secret video calls to your mobile phone, block the caller straightaway. This is **not** okay. In both cases, you can tell a trusted adult or report the person to the police.

Finally ...

Now you are growing older, your body and your life will be constantly changing. New relationships may begin and older ones may end. This next stage of your life can be both exciting and challenging. To keep yourself and others around you safe, remember all you have learnt in this book, and remember if you ever feel unsure or unsafe **do not** try to cope on your own. Make sure you talk to a trusted adult or friend, or contact Childline 1098. There is **ALWAYS** help available.

And remember:

**Your body!
Your rules!**

ACTIVITY PAGE

Write down the main things
you have learnt from this book.

Write down at least three things you can do
if you feel unsafe.

Where Can I Get Help?

Your body. Your safety.

What You Need to Know

If someone touches your private parts, asks to see or photograph your private parts, or asks you to touch their private parts, or shows you pictures of private parts, or experience an unsafe touch, you need to do three things

1. You need to say in a loud, strong voice "**No! Stop!**"

2. You need to go quickly to a trusted adult.

3. You need to tell them what happened. You may need to tell another trusted adult too.

Sometimes, the person doing these bad things to you may threaten to hurt you, your siblings or your family and friends. But don't be afraid. Follow the three steps. There are good people who will protect you.

When you experience an unsafe touch, you may feel bad, confused and helpless. Remember, don't feel bad because what happened is not your fault. It doesn't matter what some people may say. **IT IS NOT YOUR FAULT**.

Don't worry if they take this to the police. They must. They need to do this to protect you. If they don't report it, they will be in trouble too.

If you feel they are not complaining to the right people, you can complain to the police directly too.

You can also call 1098 (ChildLine) from any phone to complain or if you feel you're in danger. This is free.

You can also place a complaint at the POCSO e-box at www.ncpcr.gov.in

If you are required to place an official complaint, you must remember that a trusted adult can be with you. You don't need to go to a Police Station. They should come to your house. And usually, a policewoman will come to meet you.

A doctor may be required to check you to make sure you're fine. You have the right to ask for a trusted adult to be with you. If you're a girl, only a female doctor may check you or there should be a lady from the hospital/clinic in the room with you too.

You don't have to talk to anyone whom you are not comfortable talking about it to. You needn't talk to the media. No one can and should force you.

And most importantly, your identity will be kept secret from the public.

The Protection of Children from Sexual Offences (POCSO) Act and Rules, 2012

The Government of India is committed to protecting children like you.

In order to protect you specifically from offences of sexual assault, sexual harassment and pornography, The Protection of Children from Sexual Offences (POCSO) Act and Rules, 2012 was enacted.

The POCSO Act, 2012 keeps your interests as most important at every step of the legal process.

The POCSO Act, 2012 defines as all persons under the age of 18 as children.

Both boys and girls are vulnerable to such attacks and The POCSO Act, 2012 protects all children.

The POCSO Act, 2012 includes and recognises all possible sexual crimes and sexual exploitation of children.

The POCSO Act, 2012 includes simple and child-friendly processes and systems for reporting, recording evidence, investigation and quick trials of offences through Special Courts just for you.

The National Commission for Protection of Child Rights (NCPCR) is mandated to monitor the implementation of POCSO Act, 2012.

Notes for Educators

The following notes are designed to be used with teachers and counsellors to help young people unpack the messages in this book. An important aspect of these notes is that students are encouraged to discuss issues openly and honestly, and without fear of embarrassment or ridicule. Support students through these discussions by being helpful and empathetic. There will be no right answers. When students do speak up, it may be a brave thing for them to do, especially in front of their peers; so ensure you are encouraging and kind towards them at all times. This book has been designed to be used over a number of sessions.

Note: if at any time a student begins to disclose, stop them gently and say, 'What you have to tell me is very important. We can talk about this after the lesson, then I can give you my full attention.' Ensure they know you are concerned and value what they are about to reveal. If another teacher is available, have them continue the lesson and take the student aside so they can disclose in a safe environment. Protective interrupting is important so confidentially is kept and it prevents other students from hearing the disclosure. If a child does disclose, never deal with the disclosure by yourself; contact xxxxxx{SHANTHI }

It takes an enormous amount of courage for a child (or adult) to disclose abuse of any type. To find the bravery to overcome such threats is a true act of courage. But what a student needs more than anything from the person they disclose to — be it a parent, relative, teacher or friend — is compassionate reassurance. Therefore, stay calm and:

- reassure the student you believe them
- reassure the student they have done the right thing in telling
- reassure the student that they are incredibly brave and courageous
- reassure the student that they are in NO way to blame
- reassure the student that they are loved
- reassure the student that they are safe and will be looked after
- reassure the student that you will do everything you can to stop the abuse (never promise it will stop)
- contact one of the organisations listed on pages 60 to 61.

Introduction (page v)

Introduce this book to students by reading the Introduction to or with them. Ask, 'How do you keep your body safe? Do you think it is more difficult for girls to keep their body safe than boys?' Discuss. Ask, 'What does "respect" mean to you?' Write down students' ideas on the board or on poster paper, and refer to these as you work through the book. Reinforce that all children have the right to be safe and that this is part of the UN Convention on the Rights of the Child (explore this document if time allows). However, sometimes children are unable to protect this right and this is where they need the help of trusted adults. Write the last sentence from page v on the board or display on poster paper in the classroom.

Page 1

After reading the text, ask, 'How is your body changing? How about your emotions, are they always changing from day to day?' Discuss. Ask, 'What is puberty?' Discuss students' answers.

Pages 2–5

Discuss the text in this section in a practical way. If students become uncomfortable, embarrassed or start to joke around, reinforce that puberty and the changes that come with it are both normal and natural. If boys and girls are finding the discussion challenging, then separate them into gendered groups. However, it saying that, it is very important that both boys and girls understand these changes from each other's perspective, and therefore develop a better understanding and compassion for what the opposite gender may be going through. Ask students how they feel about these changes, if they have ever received any information about puberty and who they talk to when they need information about the changes they are going through. It is important that both genders have open and honest discussions about how they are feeling so the taboos

around sexual development can be broken. View the diagrams of the internal workings of a male and female body. Discuss their function. The more information students have about their own bodies, the safer and more confident they will be. Review the meaning of private and public.

Pages 6–7

Discuss the correct terminology for private parts. Ensure there is no embarrassment or awkwardness. Inform students that if they are ever touched inappropriately, it is important they know the correct terms for their private parts because if they needed to seek police help it would be very important that they could clearly state where they were touched inappropriately. Ensure students know sex with a person under the age of 18 years is illegal in India. (Read the red circle and discuss.) However, also reinforce that when they are older and more mature, a sexual relationship with the right person where there is respect can be very rewarding. But at this stage of their lives, the best thing to do is be friends with the opposite sex and enjoy fun activities with friends such as sport.

Pages 8–9

Discuss the text on this page. Reinforce that students have the right to be safe, and that they do not always have to do what an adult tells them — especially in relation to their body. Discuss how sometimes it is hard to stand up to an adult especially if they are a person in authority. However, they must feel no guilt or shame, and they need to tell a trusted adult straightaway if they are being harmed or feel unsafe in anyway. Reinforce to students that it is their right to feel safe.

Pages 10–13

After reading the text on these pages, discuss with students what makes them angry/sad/anxious/happy, etc. If at any time a student feels upset, reassure them that they can talk to you (if you are one of their trusted adults) or a trusted adult privately about their concerns. Review how hormones are not only changing their body but also their emotions. Ask, 'Have you ever felt embarrassed? Like everyone is watching only you? Or worried and you don't know why?' Reinforce that students don't have to solve their problems on their own. There is always someone who will listen to them. Suggest your students keep a diary.

Pages 14–17

Read through the text with students. Ask, 'What do you like about yourself? What things make you feel better about yourself? Why is important to like yourself rather than rely on the compliments of others? What is unique about you?' Discuss in general terms, students' hopes and dreams for the future. Ask, 'Why is it important to have goals for the future?' Have students read through the Self-esteem Tips. Say, 'I want you to try some of these things every day for a few weeks. Then I will check in with you and see how you are feeling about yourself.' Ask students to complete activity page 17. On some paper students could also draw themselves in 10 years time and write a summary of what they hope they have achieved.

Pages 18–23

Review the seven Body Safety rules with students. Some students may have learned this information when they were younger and some may not. However, it is important all students go over these seven points again. Discuss each rule as necessary. Have students complete activity pages 22 and 23.

Pages 24–27

Discuss the two instances on page 24 where a student may find it difficult to say 'No.' Reinforce that students have rights over their bodies. Talk about how sometimes we all have to be brave but it is important to tell a trusted adult if we feel unsafe. Discuss and answer any of the questions students might have. Have students complete activity pages 26 and 27.

Pages 28–33

Before reading the text, ask, 'What do you think consent means?' List the students' ideas on the board or poster paper. Ask, 'Can you tell me about some situations when you did not give your consent and what resulted?' Discuss. Read through the text and unpack the information with the students. Reinforce that sex with a child under the age of 18 years is illegal in India and punishable by law. Examine the poster on page 38 and the text on page 30. Go through the words with the students. Have students role play asking for consent (see poster), for example, 'Can I please hold your hand?' and the various responses — both negative and positive. Ensure students understand the difference between a person happily and willingly giving their consent and not giving their consent. Ensure students understand that silence is not consent and people can withdraw consent at ANY time. Have students complete activity pages 32 and 33.

Pages 34–35

These pages will prepare a student for a time when they will have a sexual relationship later in life. Therefore, work slowly through the five points. Discuss as required and answer any questions students might have. Reassure students that being in a trusting, happy and healthy relationship when they are adults can be rewarding and wonderful but there must be respect from both partners.

Pages 36–43

Read the text on pages 36 and 37 with students. Discuss the examples provided. Talk about both verbal consent and body language where consent is not given. Ensure students understand that consent can be withdrawn at any time and just because a person consents once does not mean they will the next time. Review the two important points and discuss. Talk about how times are changing especially for woman and that they have the right to travel and work where they like without judgement. Discuss being an 'upstander' if it is safe to do so and stand up for someone who is unable to say 'No' to unwanted touch. Ensure students know they can ring the police if they (or another person) feels unsafe. Have students complete activity pages 42 and 43. Discuss each scenario on page 42. Encourage students to write any questions they might have for a class discussion or a one-on-one conference with a trusted teacher.

Pages 44–47

Read and discuss each point in detail. Talk about the pictures and the body language. As a class, summarize in point form all the elements they can recall of a caring and respectful relationship. Ask students to commit to this type of respectful relationship at school even in a friendship capacity.

Pages 48–53

Take time to unpack and discuss each checklist. If students feel safe to do so they can add examples of an abuse from their own lives. Discuss the different types of abuse as listed on these pages. Copy the four checklists and provide them to the students for their reference. Have students complete activity pages 52 and 53.

Pages 54–59

Discuss the dangers and misconceptions of pornography. Go through the DOs and DON'Ts of staying safe on the internet. Take time to listen to students' concerns and ask them questions about their own use of their mobile phone. Alert them to the idea that not everyone is who they say they are on the internet. Read the summary on page 58 and have students complete the activity on page 59.

Pages 60–61

Read pages 60 and 61. Ensure all students know where they can get help and that they are never alone; there is always an organisation or someone out there they can trust who will be able to help them get through difficult and/or unsafe times.

Notes

www.ingramcontent.com/pod-product-compliance
Lightning Source LLC
Chambersburg PA
CBHW041133170626
46815CB00009B/348